The Berenstain Bears'
FAMILY GET - TOGETHER

Stan & Jan Berenstain

A GOLDEN BOOK • NEW YORK
Western Publishing Company, Inc., Racine, Wisconsin 53404

I'm so pleased
we have good weather
for our great big family
get-together!

Who's coming to
our family party?

Cousin Jill
and Uncle Artie,
Grizzly Gramps
and Gran,
of course,
Great-Aunt Min
and Cousin Morse.

Aunts and uncles,
nephews, nieces
will come together
like puzzle pieces.

We do indeed
have good weather.
But are we *ready*
for our get-together?

6

We've done our best
to prepare
to welcome folks
to our lair.

We've borrowed chairs
from miles around.
We've had our yard
wired for sound.

8

We've lots of room
for cars to park.

We've put up lights
for when it's dark.

We have lots and lots
of food and drink.
Yes, we *are* prepared,
I think.

All coming to
our family party!
Cousin Jill
and Uncle Artie!

Grizzly Gramps
and Gran, of course!
Great-Aunt Min
and Cousin Morse!

13

Look! Twin Cousins
Mike and Ike
are riding their
two-seater bike.

Look out! Auntie Mame
and Cousin Klute
are coming down
by parachute!

15

Here come more
in cars and buses!
And a great big truck!
It's Uncle Gus's!

We shout hello!

We kiss! We hug!

We pass around

the honey jug!

Papa Bear
and Uncle Mack
slap each other
on the back.

18

We take pictures
of each other.

Here's one of me, Pa, Sis,
and Mother.

We dance. We sing.

We laugh at jokes.

It's fun to be
with family folks.

Then we eat,

and eat,

and eat,

and eat,

and eat.

Now we hear
from Great-Aunt Bess—
"All right, you bears.
Clean up this mess!"

Then all is quiet.

All is calm.

Bears line up

to thank our mom

for the family
get-together.
She gets a gift
from Cousin Heather.

We say good-bye.
We kiss. We hug.

We finish off

the honey jug.

Back into cars.

Back into buses.

Back into the truck
that's Uncle Gus's.

Our get-together
now is done.
We're glad you came,
everyone.
We hope that you had
FUN! FUN! FUN!